D1121185

Charity LARGE PRINT

(The Amish Buggy Horse, Book 3)

Ruth Hartzler

Charity LARGE PRINT
(The Amish Buggy Horse, Book 3)
Ruth Hartzler
Copyright © 2015 Ruth Hartzler
All Rights Reserved
ISBN 9781925689297

Scripture quotations are from The Holy Bible, English Standard Version® (ESV®), copyright © 2001 by Crossway, a publishing ministry of Good News Publishers. Used by permission. All rights reserved.

Quotation from *The Martyrs' Mirror* is from: John S. Oyer & Robert Kreider, *Mirror of the Martyrs: Stories of courage, inspiringly retold, of 16th century Anabaptists who gave their lives for their faith*, Good Books, 2002, pp. 36-37.

CONTENTS

CHAPTER 1

ISABEL PULLED HER HEAVY black shawl closer to her neck as she looked out the window of the little café. "It looks like the weather's getting worse out there."

Melissa, her good friend, agreed. "I'd best be getting home. Victor was worried about me coming out in this weather today."

"But we still have twenty more minutes for lunch. I don't have to be back at work for a while yet.

You don't want to stay and talk some more about your new husband?"

"Sorry, Isabel." Melissa smiled. "I could talk about Victor all day, but it doesn't look like it's getting any better out there. Anyway, you should get yourself a boyfriend, and speaking of that, what's happening with Jakob?"

Isabel sighed. "Everyone keeps telling me that he's a *gut* match for me. I suppose I'll have to get married sooner or later. I do want *kinner*."

Melissa laughed. "You're young, Isabel. There's plenty of time for *kinner*."

Isabel raised one eyebrow. "I don't know. Jakob's dependable and all that, I suppose. He'd make a *gut* husband, no doubt. There's just something missing."

"No spark?" Melissa asked as she gulped the last of her coffee and rose from the table.

Isabel's shoulders sagged and she looked out the large windows at the snow. "*Jah*, there's no spark. But what choice is there? There are no other suitable *menner* in the community."

Melissa winked at her. "You know, you might find a *mann* outside the community, like I did."

Isabel snorted rudely. "Like that's ever going to happen."

"You never know, now that you've borrowed the buggy horse, Blessing, from my *bruder*. Blessing brought Victor to me, and he brought Nettie to my *bruder*. Wait and see."

"*Ach*, you're *ab im kopp*." Isabel chuckled and gave Melissa a playful tap on the arm.

As the two parted ways, Isabel made her way back to the Old Candle Store where she worked. It was warm and cozy in the candle store, and Isabel loved the atmosphere: the scent of innumerable fragrant candles, the warm glow of candlelight, and the quaintness of the store.

On this cold, winter day, Isabel's steps quickened. The ice bit into her cheeks and she held the shawl closer to her face. She went to the parking place to check that the thick, waterproof blanket was still on Blessing, but when she got there, it was on the ground. Isabel picked it up and threw it back over Blessing, but as soon as she did, he reached around with his teeth and pulled it off.

"Blessing!" she scolded. "It's freezing. I've never known you to do that before. Here, I'll have to tighten the dees."

After the blanket was suitably adjusted, Isabel hurried back to the store. As she turned down the side street where the store was located, she noticed that no one else was braving the weather; the street was deserted. *I doubt there'll be many customers this afternoon*, she thought.

As Isabel ducked under the porch roof of the store, she noted to her surprise that the *Closed* sign was hanging inside the door. The next thing she knew, she was knocked to the ground by a man exiting the door in a rush.

The two locked eyes for a moment, and a sudden fear ran through Isabel. The man made no move to help her, but hesitated for a moment, before hurrying down the street.

Isobel looked after him with surprise. *How rude*, she thought, gingerly picking herself up off the ground. Her arm hurt where she had landed heavily on it, throwing it out to save herself. She reached for the door the second time, wondering why the *Closed* sign was hanging on it. Her boss, Mr. Harrison, always filled in for her when she went to lunch.

Isabel walked through the door, flipping the sign to *Open*. Mr. Harrison was not behind the front counter—perhaps he'd been called out on an urgent errand. *Jah, that must be it*, Isabel thought, a little puzzled as to what could be so urgent that her boss couldn't wait for her to return from lunch.

Isabel stuck her head around the door of the back room to see if Mr. Harrison was there, but there was no sign of him. She was about to take up her place at the front counter when something at floor level through the open office door caught her eye.

Isabel looked again. To her shock and distress, she saw a pair of legs. Isabel ran over to Mr. Harrison, who was lying on the ground. At first she was too shocked to notice the pool of blood. Isabel clutched at her head, and then ran to the store phone to call 911.

CHAPTER 2

ISABEL SAT NUMBLY in a chair on the far side of the Old Candle Store, while paramedics and police scurried around like ants. Isabel averted her eyes when Mr. Harrison was wheeled out, a bag completely covering him. She could hear Mrs. Harrison sobbing loudly from the residence above the store.

Isabel was disorientated and dizzy. It was if she were watching a scene unfold before her eyes, a scene that she was watching from afar. Nothing made any sense. Her eyes fell on a handsome man in a dark suit talking to a photographer.

The man at once walked over to her and sat opposite. "I'm Detective Stutzman." He took off his coat, and draped it over the back of his chair.

"Where are you taking Mr. Harrison?"

The detective frowned. "To a local hospital. You do realize he's deceased?"

Isabel was at once annoyed. Did the man think she was an idiot? "Of course I do," she snapped, but then added, "I'm sorry, it's such a shock."

If Isabel had expected sympathy in the man's gray eyes, she got none. "Do you mind if I tape this?"

A wave of dizziness washed over Isabel and she clutched at her stomach.

"Did you hear what I said?" The detective was peering at her.

Isabel noted his square jaw, his dark short hair, and his broad shoulders, and then wondered why she would notice such things in these circumstances.

Isabel nodded, although she had not, in fact, heard what he said after he asked if he may tape the interview.

"Your name?"

No sooner had Isabel said, "Isabel Slabaugh," than the man barked, "Full name? Date of birth? I don't suppose you have a home telephone number?"

Isabel winced, but answered clearly.

"What is your relationship to the deceased?"

Isabel was appalled. "I did not have a relationship with Mr. Harrison," she said, highly offended. "He was married, and is old enough to be my *grossdawdi*." A tear trickled out her eye and she swiftly wiped it away with the back of her hand.

The detective sighed and shook his head. "That just means - how did you know him?"

"Oh." Isabel was embarrassed, and her ears burned with humiliation.

"I worked for Mr. Harrison and his wife, Peggy."

"You work here?" the detective asked her, and she nodded. "Please do not nod or otherwise use gestures, as this is being recorded." He nodded to the tape machine whirring away on the table next to him. "Do you work here? For how long?" His tone was stern.

"Yes. Seven years," Isabel said, after adding them quickly up in her head. It hadn't felt like that long. Saying it out aloud, thinking that she had worked for Mr. Harrison for so long, almost a decade really, made her tear up again. Stinging tears fell down her cheeks. Detective Stutzman reached into his inner coat pocket and pulled out a handkerchief. He handed it to her and Isabel took it, dabbing her eyes with a corner of the silky material.

"What about the other employees? Are you working alone today?"

"There are no other employees, only me," Isabel said.

"Did the deceased and Mrs. Harrison work in the store too?"

Isabel winced when the detective referred to Mr. Harrison as *the deceased*. "No, Mrs. Harrison didn't work here, but Mr. Harrison did when I was off."

The detective stroked his chin and narrowed his eyes. "So money was tight for them? Did Mr. Harrison have a life insurance policy?"

Isabel's mouth fell open. Was the detective thinking that Peggy killed her husband for money? She was suddenly afraid, thrust into a world of *Englischers* who were suspicious. She stood up.

Detective Stutzman spoke quickly, and with such a tone in his voice that it frightened Isabel for a moment. "Sit down," he said. "I'm not done."

Isabel dropped back into her seat.

Stutzman continued. "What about you? He must not be able to pay you too much."

"I live with my parents," Isabel said.

"How old are you?" Stutzman asked.

"Twenty-two," Isabel answered.

"And you've worked here for seven years?"

Isabel nodded, but then remembered she was not allowed to nod, and said, "Yes."

The detective stopped for a moment to speak to a police officer. "Yes, you deal with the two deputy county coroners and I'll continue to interview Miss Slabaugh. See to it that I'm not disturbed *this* time."

The man scurried away.

The detective turned the tape machine back on. "Please describe the circumstances to me in which you found the body."

Isabel described what happened from the time she approached the store door to the time she found Mr. Harrison. The detective did not speak until she had finished. "Describe the man again, please," he said.

Isabel was puzzled. "But you're recording it," she said, pointing to the tape.

The detective raised his eyebrows, so Isabel pushed on, before he could chastise her again.

"He was short, and seemed very strong looking, like a farmer used to hard work." The detective raised his eyebrows again at that one, but she continued. "His lips were wide, and he had one eye closed. His hair was brown but graying. He had a tiny, little beard."

"Go on."

"His left eye was almost closed, as if he'd had an old injury."

Detective Stutzman nodded as he scribbled words down in his notebook. When Isobel was done he stood up. "Thank you for your time. We'll be in touch about when to come to the station to give your statement. You may go," he added, and then spun around and hurried away.

He spoke to another detective in a corner and Isabel overheard the words, "No discrepancies." She hoped that was a good thing.

Isabel sat in shock. She had not expected the conversation to be over so quickly. She disliked the detective's manner, but there was something appealing about him. As Isabel walked out the front door of the store, she could feel the detective's eyes burning into her back.

* * *

Stutzman watched the young woman for a minute, and then he cranked the key, and the engine of his dark blue sedan roared to life. He put the car in drive and pulled out into the street, away from the curb. He fell in with traffic and drove a few blocks before parking at the curb once more, this time in front of a little café. He climbed out his car and went in, standing in a short line before ordering a coffee. He took the steaming mug to a table and sat by the window.

He always did that, pondering over a case with the help of a hot cup of coffee. It was as if he needed the caffeine to help him think. After his conversation with Isabel, he was sure the woman hadn't known anything about the murder, and he was reasonably sure Harrison hadn't gotten himself killed, and his wife hadn't killed him either.

But that left no one. No other suspects. The wife was a bad suspect, Harrison himself was a bad suspect, and Isabel was too naive and innocent to have planned anything. Besides, she was Amish. Stutzman shuddered. But if it wasn't one of them, who was it? Stutzman didn't have an answer. One thing was for sure; the girl was lucky that she had tended to her horse before returning to the Old Candle Store. Otherwise, there would have likely been two victims.

Why the thought of harm coming to the Amish woman upset him so much, he did not know. He had felt an instant attraction to her, but figured that was just some lingering effects of his past.

Nevertheless, he felt an almost primal urge to protect her.

He drank his steaming coffee while he looked out the window, watching cars pass by, and people walk up and down the street. His stomach rumbled and he stood and returned to the counter to get a refill and buy a croissant. He sat at the same table to eat his food. Afterwards, he left his mug on the table on top of a small tip for whoever cleaned it up, and went outside.

His next move was to interview Peggy Harrison, but the

paramedics had refused to allow him to speak to her at the scene. After that, he wasn't sure who else he could talk to. The Harrisons did not have children; in fact, neither of them had any surviving family outside of Peggy's sister. Once again the engine roared to life and Stutzman pulled his car onto the street.

CHAPTER 3

ISABEL COULD NOT SLEEP. She could not sleep because she had just a few days ago seen her boss's body on the store floor. She had then had been subjected to a grueling questioning when she had given her statement to a woman police officer at the police station.

The scene was burned into her brain, and it had been replaying in her mind's eye over and over as she lay in bed and watched the sky grow darker, and then lighter. Now it was Monday morning and she had to return to the Old Candle Store. The sun was almost clear of the horizon, and yellow light streamed into her room through the window next to the bed.

No one spoke to her at breakfast, but her parents shot her worried looks. She was glad they had not mentioned the murder to her over the weekend—she had no desire to talk to anyone about it, not just yet. Her *mudder* had been worried about her, and had checked in on her once or twice each night, but she had pretended to be asleep.

Isabel had been concerned about returning to the Old Candle Store. She had no idea if it would even be open today, but there had been no word to the contrary from Mrs. Harrison.

Isabel drove Blessing to the small lot beside the squat, red brick store that seemed crammed into the busy main street of downtown. She tied him well, and put his thick, winter blanket over him. She picked her way across little bits of yellow police tape lying outside the door, and unlocked the door with her old, silver key. When she went in, she shut the door behind her and flipped over the placard that sat in the small, square door window, changing it from *Closed* to *Open*.

Isabel moved to the checkout counter. She turned on the electronic till, and opened the drawer, only to see that there was no money in it. She would have to go to her boss's office, in the back of the store. She had a key to that as well, but she had been dreading going there, and was hoping she wouldn't have to do so that day.

She walked along the rows of candles, trailing a fingertip along a wooden shelf, and then she was at the small brown door that had a card stating, *Office*, in big, black, blocky letters. She slid the office key into the lock and turned it. The door swung open, and once again Isabel was crying.

The office was small, and had a long desk with a chair behind it, and two chairs sitting in front of it. Dear Mr. Harrison had been an avid reader, and his office showed that. He had several books strewn over his desk, with the one he had currently been reading sitting in front of his chair with a slip of white paper as a bookmark.

Isabel reached over to look at the cover of the book. It was a murder mystery. Isabel dropped it back on the desk in horror. It seemed like a cruel joke.

The shrill ringing of the phone made Isabel jump. She trembled, and held the phone to her ear. "Hello?" Her voice was shaky.

"Hello dear," a woman's voice said. It was Peggy, Mr. Harrison's wife. She had little to do with the day to

day running of the Old Candle
Store, but, as the Harrisons lived
above the store, Isabel knew
Peggy quite well.

Isabel was the only person who
worked in the candle store, along
with Mr. Harrison. When she was
at lunch, he was there, and if he
took a day off, she replaced him.
Isabel vaguely wondered what
would happen now.

"Hello, dear," the voice said again.

"How are you?" Isabel asked softly,
a wave of pity and sadness
washing over her.

"I'm not good, my dear," Peggy said. "I'm in bed and staying with my sister, or I would've come over to see you."

Isabel had always liked Peggy Harrison. She was as short and skinny as a rail, with a mound of white hair upon her head. She was in her seventies now, much like her husband had been. It seemed crazy to Isabel that someone would murder a seventy something year old man, and she was still having trouble coming to terms with the fact that someone had.

"I'm staying with my sister," Peggy

said again. "I can't close the store though. I don't know if my husband ever told you, but things are tight."

Isabel had, in fact, been aware of the situation. The store was the only thing the couple had, and sales had been falling steadily for a decade. It seemed that not many people wanted candles any more, and half those who did, purchased them online. Nevertheless, Isabel did not think it would be polite to tell Mrs. Harrison that she knew all about their money problems, so she stayed quiet and let her continue.

"I can't run the store anyways," Peggy continued. "I never learned much about it."

Isabel waited until Peggy's voice trailed off and then spoke. "I can keep it open for you."

There was a pregnant pause from the other side of the phone, and when Peggy spoke again, her voice betrayed the fact that she was close to tears. Isabel figured that Peggy Harrison had been crying for most of the night.

"I'll come over and see you later,

when I feel a little better. I just wanted to know if you can keep the store open until I sort things out. I'm going to stay with my sister until I feel better. Then I'll probably have to close the store, but I can't think straight at the moment. Would you be able to keep it open just another few days, please?"

"Yes, of course," Isabel said. She had no idea what to say to Peggy, despite her urge to reassure her.

She walked around the desk, and then lowered herself into the ancient chair that Mr. Harrison had favored. She bent, and used the same key she had used on the door to unlock a drawer. There was a key there to a safe built into the wall behind her, and she opened it and pulled out a stack of money. She counted out the correct bill for an opening shift till, and then locked everything back up.

Isabel hurried out of the office, pulling it shut behind her, and locking it. She returned to the front, and was putting the money into the till when she heard the small silver bell above the front door ding as the door opened.

* * *

Detective Peter Stutzman sighed when he saw the Amish girl's startled face. He supposed she thought it might have been the murderer returning, and then what would she have done? Absolutely nothing, as he knew only too well. For some reason he had a strange urge to hug her and tell her everything would be all right, but he quickly dismissed that as a peculiarity caused by the stress of his occupation.

"Hello, Miss Slabaugh." Before she could speak, he pressed on. "I just have a few more questions about the man's description."

"But I've told you already," Isabel said, "and I gave a statement at the police station, too."

Detective Stutzman sighed. Why did witnesses always complain? He was only doing his job. "Please describe the man to me again." He watched as a flash of annoyance passed across Isabel's face, followed by a look of resignation.

"He was short and well built. I'd say he was around fifty years of age. His hair was brown with a lot of gray though it. He had a hard face. One of his eyes was closed, almost closed anyway."

"Which eye was that?"

"His left eye."

"Are you sure?'

"Yes."

Detective Stutzman rubbed his chin. What was of interest was the fact that Isabel had described Clifton Raines perfectly. Raines had been a criminal with a long rap sheet, and, many years ago, it had been Mr. Harrison's testimony that had sent him to jail. Raines had been released on bail only two weeks before the murder.

Stutzman had found this out pretty quickly, but Raines had claimed to be with his lawyer, and not just any lawyer at that, but a well known criminal lawyer. The lawyer had corroborated Raines' claim, and had even produced a video, complete with time stamp, showing Raines entering his office before the murder, and leaving long after it. It was a pretty tight alibi, and so Stutzman could see no reason to concentrate on Raines.

"We'd like you come down to the

station to do an Identi-Kit picture of the man you saw."

"What's that?" Isabel's forehead furrowed in confusion.

"You describe the man to, well, an artist of sorts, and he puts together a picture of the man. We use that picture to help us identify him."

"Oh." Isabel looked thoughtful. "Yes, I can go tomorrow morning, if Mrs. Harrison will give me the time off."

Stutzman was taken aback. Surely the girl didn't intend to keep the store open after a serious crime had been committed here? "I don't think you understand," he said slowly. "This was an execution-style murder, and I don't think it's advisable to be here at all. Mrs. Harrison is staying with her sister, so she's out of harm's way, and I suggest you go home and keep well away from here."

To his annoyance, the girl simply shrugged. "I'm sure I'm in no danger," she said.

"You witnessed a man fleeing from the scene of the murder," Stutzman said. He was rapidly losing patience. "You said the man saw you, so he knows you're an eye witness, and you're the *only* eye witness. You could be in grave danger."

"*Gott* will protect me, if it is His will," she said.

Stutzman was furious. He turned on his heel and left, without another word.

CHAPTER 4

WHEN ISABEL ARRIVED home that afternoon, her parents were sitting at the big kitchen table. She joined them, and after the silent prayer, her *mudder* hopped up. "Isabel, I've made you Dutch Goose, your favorite." She hurried to the stove and soon returned, and then spooned two inch slices of piping hot Dutch Goose onto a plate, and then covered it with gravy made out of the drippings.

Isabel thanked her mother and then reached for a jug of water, but her *mudder* beat her to it, reaching across the table and snatching the jug. She poured Isabel a glass and handed it to her.

"*Denki*," Isabel said, "but please don't feel you have to do everything for me. I'm fine, really."

"You are not fine," her *mudder* said. "How could you say that? You saw something terrible."

"If she says she's fine, she's fine," her father said in a quiet voice. Isabel could tell he was thinking about something, and it piqued her interest.

"What are you thinking about, *Datt*?"

"I'm just reliving something," he said. He stayed quiet for a moment, but his daughter knew him well, and knew he would presently launch into his story. It was a story her *mudder* must have known, because she leaned forward and spoke to her husband in a hushed tone.

"Do *not* tell her this."

"It could help her," Mr. Slabaugh

said, waving off his *fraa* by swinging a hand in the air. He turned to Isabel. "When I was a younger *mann*, I had married your *mudder*, and you were just a *boppli*."

Mrs. Slabaugh sighed and stood, took her empty plate to the sink, and dropped it inside with a bang.

"It was winter, and I was driving down a desolate stretch of road. I don't know what made me look, but I just happened to glance out my window right at the perfect moment to see a red glow coming from down the side of an embankment. It was night, and dark as could be. It was snowing lightly then, but it had been coming down really good earlier that day. I pulled my horse to the side and stopped. By the time I had gotten the horse stopped, being careful in the snow and everything, I was a little distance away. I pulled my coat around me, and I walked back."

Mrs. Slabaugh walked back and sat down, and put her hand on her husband's shoulder.

"Sure enough there was a car down there," he continued. "There was a dip off the road, and it continued to a stand of trees. I made my way down the hill and got to the car. There was a *mann* in the car. Now, this was a time before cell phones or any of that, or perhaps it was the early days of them, I don't know, but he did not have a cell phone that I could use to call for help. I took one look at the *mann* and I turned to go back to my buggy to rush for help, but in a small voice he asked me not to."

Isabel's father took a moment, sipped his meadow tea, and then continued.

"He knew no one would come in time, and I knew it as well. So I stayed. I stood next to him and I opened the door and reached in to hold his hand. He looked at me. He knew it was coming; he closed his eyes, and a tear rolled down his cheek. Our breaths were coming out in blasts of fog, until finally his wasn't coming anymore. Then I went to the road, where a truck had stopped at the sight of my horse tied to a tree. He went on for help, and eventually the police came out there."

Isabel looked at her *vadder* for a long time. She did not know what to say. They sat quietly and then finally Isabel thought of something. When she spoke, her voice was wavering. "Did it keep you up at night?"

Her *vadder* looked to her. He took another sip, and then he nodded. "*Jah*," he said. "It did."

"Does it now?"

"*Nee.*"

"How did you start sleeping?"

The older man shrugged. "The *mann* asked me to pray with him.

He left his physical body, and I hope he went to be with *Gott*. These physical bodies are just clothes, nothing but clothes that we shed when we go to be with *Gott*. Here, pass me the *Martyrs Mirror*."

Isabel walked into the living room to fetch the *Martyrs Mirror*, a heavy, thousand page book owned by many Amish. It contained the story of over eight hundred Anabaptist martyrs who were imprisoned and then executed for their belief in adult baptism around four hundred years ago. In fact, at that time, many thousands of Christians were persecuted for their belief in adult baptism.

Isabel knew what was coming; her *vadder* had one particular story he always liked to read, that of the martyr Dirk Willems. As so Isabel sat at the kitchen table while her *vadder* once again read to her the story of Dirk Willems. In 1569, Willems escaped from his prison cell and fled across a frozen moat. No sooner had he made it safely across, than the guard who was chasing him, fell through the ice and sank into the icy water. Not wanting the man to die, Dirk Willems at once hurried back and pulled the guard to safety. Despite the fact that he had saved the guard's life, Dirk Willems was executed by being burned at the stake.

"And so," Mr. Slabaugh concluded, "Dirk Willems showed compassion for his enemy. He did not repay evil with evil."

Isabel expected her father to close the huge book, as he always did at this point, but he tapped the page and reread the first section:

"In the year 1569 a pious, faithful brother and follower of Jesus Christ, named Dirk Willems, was apprehended at Asperen, in Holland, and had to endure severe tyranny from the papists. But as he had founded his faith not upon the drifting sand of human commandments, but upon the firm foundation stone, Christ Jesus, he, notwithstanding all evil winds of human doctrine, and heavy showers of tyrannical and severe persecution, remained immovable and steadfast unto the end; wherefore, when the chief Shepherd shall appear in the clouds of heaven and gather together His elect from all the ends of the earth, he shall also through grace hear the words, 'Well done, good and faithful servant; thou hast been faithful over a few things, I will make thee ruler over many things; enter thou into the joy of thy Lord.'"

"Death is the will of *Gott*," her *vadder* continued. "Who are we to know the will of *Gott*? Death holds no fear for us. Remember Ecclesiastes chapter three, which says, '*For everything there is a season, and a time for every matter under heaven: a time to be born, and a time to die.*"

Isabel nodded. Her father got up and took his dishes to the sink. He came back to the table, stood beside his daughter, and put his hand on her shoulder. He squeezed her arm, and then he left the kitchen.

CHAPTER 5

ISABEL PULLED BLESSING to a stop in front of the police station and took a deep breath. She knew why she felt nervous, and it had nothing to do with the investigation, and everything to do with being in close proximity to Detective Stutzman. She had no idea why, but she had felt an instant attraction to him, and he had been on her mind ever since. He made her heart race and her stomach churn. It was foolish to have such silly thoughts, especially over an *Englischer*. Why, the *mann* probably hardly even knew she was alive, and even if he did, he would never be interested in an Amish girl. And even if he happened to be, there was no hope of any future for an Amish with an *Englischer*. Such marriages were strictly *verboten*.

"Come on," Isabel said to herself, taking one more breath and then climbing down from the buggy. There was a loud honk as a car in the street swerved to avoid the buggy. Isabel buried her face in her hands. She had to stop thinking about the detective. He was an *Englischer*, she told herself for the umpteenth time, but there was simply something about the detective that she admired.

Isobel tied Blessing to the rail in the place reserved for buggy parking. She hurried to the sidewalk and then to the front door of the station. Inside the station was a small lobby with faded linoleum flooring that could stand to be washed, and a long, tall desk manned by a stern-looking woman with a sharp face and short black hair.

"Hello," Isabel said to the woman as she stopped at the desk. "My name is Isobel Slabaugh. I'm here to see Detective Stutzman."

The woman looked up briefly, punched some keys on her computer, then nodded and opened a drawer. She pulled out a name tag that could be stuck to Isabel's over-apron. Instead of a name, the word *Visitor* was printed across a line in thick black letters. She handed it to Isabel. "Third floor."

With that, the woman looked back down at her computer, leaving

Isabel to head to the elevators by herself. She stepped into the small box and pressed the button for the third floor. The doors slid closed in front of her and the compartment started moving upwards. There was a soft ding after it came to a stop, and the door slid open.

The third floor was a mostly open room, with desks placed in two rows within it. Men and women moved this way and that; some sat at the desks, talking on phones and typing on keyboards. It was monochrome, all gray with white desks. Isabel smoothed her apron and stepped out of the elevator. She stood there a moment, scanning the room, trying to spot Detective Stutzman.

Finally, she saw him near the back, leaning against a desk and speaking with an older man who was sitting at the desk. The older man had thinning white hair and a big belly that he barely managed to keep contained behind the desk. Isabel moved away from the elevator, weaving her way through the crowd of detectives and police officers until she came to stand behind Stutzman.

She reached out and tapped him on the shoulder. He spun, a laugh fading from his lips.

"Oh, hello, Miss Slabaugh." His tone was less formal this time. Stutzman turned and spoke to the other man. "Don't forget the rest of that joke, Jake," he said. "I have something to take care of."

Jake nodded and reached for the half eaten candy bar sitting on his desk. Detective Stutzman turned back to Isabel and then jerked his head to the side, as if to indicate *follow me*. Isabel nodded and let herself be led across the room, to a much tidier desk. The detective sat behind it and she took a seat on a small fold out chair across from him.

"Now, please describe the man to me again."

"Again?" Isabel's voice rose. "Again? But I've described him a thousand times already. I described him in that report you read."

"Humor me, will you?" Stutzman said. His tone was now icy.

Isabel looked down at a photo on the detective's desk. It looked just like the man she had seen, judging from the brief glimpse, but the detective snatched it up and put it in a drawer. "You've found him, haven't you?" Isabel asked.

The detective rubbed his chin. "We did find a man fitting the description you gave," he said slowly and carefully, "but it wasn't him."

"It has to be him. Who else could it be? I'm sure not too many people look like that," Isabel said. The conversation was just starting and she was already feeling frustrated. "I want to see him," she said. "May

I see the picture?"

Detective Stutzman raised his hand and shook his head. "Actually, I had you come in today because, as I mentioned to you already, I want to have you sit down with a profile artist. Give him the description, and let's see what the two of you can come up with."

"I gave you the description already," Isabel said, her annoyance levels rising.

"I know, but I need you to work with the Identi-Kit detective. He'll put what you say into some computer software, and then we will get a really good understanding of what the guy looked like," Stutzman said.

"And you didn't want me to see that photo because you think I'll say that's him, whether it is or not."

The detective squirmed. "Right."

Isabel crossed her arms and leaned back in her chair, sending a cold gaze across the desk to the detective. How could she be simultaneously attracted to him and angered by him? "Why don't you believe me?"

Peter Stutzman leaned back as well, but not in anger. He took a breath. "He has a solid alibi. More than solid, it's airtight. He was with his lawyer. We have the lawyer confirming, and some other things I can't tell you about."

"You can't tell me some things?" Isabel said, her voice rising. "My boss was murdered, and there are some things you can't tell me?"

CHAPTER 6

DETECTIVE STUTZMAN STOOD UP. He raised his hands in a show of surrender. "Let's go see the Identi-Kit detective, okay? Talk to him, hash some things out, and let's see what you come up with."

Isabel was exasperated. She knew what she had seen. "But what if I come up with a picture that looks exactly like the *mann* that you're so sure is innocent? What then?"

Stutzman shrugged. "I don't know.

Let's see what we get first."

With that, he turned and walked away, beckoning for Isabel to follow. She followed him down a bare corridor until they came to another room. Inside was a desk, and at it sat a man bending over a computer.

The man at the desk, another detective, stood up at once. "My name is Scott," the man said, before Detective Stutzman could make the introductions. He had a shock of wiry red hair and a thin face with a nose that was just a tad too long for the rest of his features. His eyes were a brilliant blue, and his smile was large and welcoming. Isabel liked him at once.

"I'm Isabel," she said, leaning forward and shaking the man's offered hand.

"Great, let's get started, shall we? Come and sit in this chair beside me." He patted a plastic chair.

"Sure."

Stutzman butted in. "I'll go back to my desk. Buzz me when you're finished, Scott?"

"Sure." After the detective walked

away, Scott turned to Isabel.
"Now, I'll explain how this works.
This is facial composite software.
By the time we're finished, it will
give us a highly realistic, photo-
accurate, facial composition
picture. It will do skin tone,
everything, you name it."

Isabel felt a bit sick on the
stomach. Could she even
remember the man's skin tone?
She wasn't sure. Yet Scott proved
to be encouraging, and soon
helped put her mind to rest. Isabel
found it hard going at first, but
presently became used to the

process. They progressed through the features until they came to the eyes.

"Okay," Scott said with a nod as his hands punched in keys. Isabel leaned over the desk to watch. "How is this right eye?"

"A little wider, but not much," she said.

With a sweep of his mouse, Scott made it wider and Isabel nodded. "Then the other one, the left one was almost closed."

This part of the composite seemed to take longer, but finally Isabel

was satisfied with the result.
"Perfect," she said. "And his lips, they were thick and wide. And he had a beard, just a little narrow one, just on his chin."

"A goatee?"

Isabel was puzzled, until Scott showed her something on the screen.

"Yes," she exclaimed, "just like that. His hair was very short and dark, although it had a lot of gray through it."

After a while, Scott indicated the picture on the screen. "Like that?"

"Exactly like that."

And it went on like that for nearly a half hour, after which Isabel was astounded at the likeness. Scott summoned Detective Stutzman, who returned shortly. He stood by the desk, bending over the screen. He looked at it for a long moment, while Isabel searched his face for any information she could glean.

Had she described the man she was sure was guilty, or was she way off? She knew the image looked remarkably similar to the man she had seen, so similar in fact, that she had the chills.

Stutzman sighed. He sat in the chair opposite and sighed again.

"What is it? Is it him?" Isabel asked, leaning forward.

Stutzman held out the photograph to her. "It's Raines," he said, with resignation.

"Raines?" she said.

"I shouldn't have said his name, but his face is already all over television. The media's already all over this." He was addressing Scott, who nodded his agreement.

Isabel looked at the photograph. She reached out slowly, and took it up between her fingertips. As their fingertips touched, a jolt ran thought Isabel. She looked up at Peter, who flushed and looked away. *He felt it too*, she thought, puzzled.

Isabel forced her attention back to the photograph. The resemblance was uncanny. Isabel assumed it was an old photograph, as the man looked much younger in it, but there was no doubt in her mind that it was, in fact, the very same man. His hair was much thicker in the old photo and there were fewer lines on his face, but the wide mouth, and especially the partially closed left eye, left her in no doubt whatsoever.

"I told you," Isabel said quietly, as she set the photograph back upon the desk.

"It can't be him." The detective shook his head in disbelief.

Isabel sighed. She pursed her lips, then breathed deeply through her nose and closed her eyes for a moment. When she opened them, she saw the detective was looking right at her.

"What aren't you telling me?" she

asked him.

"It's just that he has an iron clad alibi."

Isabel stood up. "It's him. That proves it. I don't know anything about the police stuff, but you need to figure out a way to catch that man."

The detective stood as well, but he shook his head. "This isn't television. It doesn't work like that."

Isabel looked at him. "I don't watch television," she said. "I'm Amish, obviously," and then she turned and made her way to the elevator.

*   *   *

The detective watched her go. He nodded to Scott, and then returned to his desk. He didn't want to be around people at the moment.

The Amish woman infuriated him, but at the same time, there was no denying the pull he felt towards her. *Is this your doing, God?* he silently asked. Then he chuckled aloud. His job had made him so paranoid that he even thought that God Himself was plotting against him. Yet he had to admit that he was heading in a certain direction with his life, and maybe God was in fact pushing him along a little faster.

He scratched his head, and then headed for the coffee room. Thankfully, no one was there. He poured himself a stale, over-brewed coffee while the aged drip filter machine hissed at him, seemingly annoyed to be put to work.

The detective returned to his desk and tried to do some paperwork, but the image of the beautiful

Isabel Slabaugh would not leave his mind.

CHAPTER 7

WHEN ISABEL RETURNED from work that afternoon, she was concerned to see a car outside her *haus*. She looked around, but could not see anyone, so took Blessing into the barn, unharnessed him, and tended to him.

When she came out, there was still no one in sight, so she hurried into the warmth of the *haus*. There, sitting in the living room looking very much at home, was Detective

Peter Stutzman. What's more, he was tucking into a plate of pumpkin whoopie pies with cream cheese filling as he leaned back into the comfortable but worn sofa.

"You're home." Her *mudder* beamed at her. Isabel, however, noticed that her *vadder's* face was solemn.

"Hello, Detective Stutzman."

"Call me Peter, please."

Isabel's heart fluttered more earnestly. She looked around the room for somewhere to sit. The obvious place would be next to the detective, but Isabel was nervous enough already. Her *vadder* decided for her. "Sit down, Isabel," he said, pointing to the sofa.

Isabel went to the sofa and sat down, glad that there was room for three people. She sat up the furthest end to get as far as she could from the attractive detective, and leaned against the thick arm of the sofa.

"Now, Isabel," Mr. Slabaugh said, "Peter has brought locks for all our doors and windows and has spent quite some time fitting them all."

Isabel's jaw fell open. Locks on the doors? Whatever would happen next? No Amish in the community had locks on their doors. And for how long had her *vadder* and the detective been on a first name basis?

Her *vadder* was still talking. "Peter has been telling us about the situation, and he advises us that you shouldn't go to the store anymore."

"But, *Datt*," Isabel spluttered, and would have said more, but her *vadder* held up his hand. "*Nee*, it is for the best, Isabel."

"But what about Mrs. Harrison?" Isabel knew that it would be disrespectful to argue with her *vadder*, but she was concerned for Peggy Harrison who had asked her to keep the store open.

Peter Stutzman turned to her. "I've spoken to Mrs. Harrison and advised her of the circumstances, and she fully agrees that the store must remain shut until this all blows over."

"But she needs the money," Isabel said in a small voice.

Peter simply shrugged. "Mrs.

Harrison told me that she was thinking of selling the store and her apartment, and living permanently with her sister."

And so that was that. Isabel was more than a little annoyed that the handsome Peter Stutzman had gone behind her back and gone straight to her parents to get their support. The three of them were taking sides against her. Worse still, her parents seemed to be getting on very well with the detective.

"Peter also says you must carry a cell phone." Her *vadder's* voice was firm.

A cell phone? Her voice rose with dismay. Isabel looked from her *vadder* to her *mudder*, but they were both expressionless. "But we're not allowed to have cell phones."

Peter Stutzman waved one hand expressively. "That's okay, I've cleared it with the bishop. He agrees that you need to have a cell phone with you at all times due to the seriousness of the situation."

Isabel again looked from one parent to another, but this time they were both nodding. "*Datt, Mamm*, surely you can't agree with this?" she asked them.

"It's for your own safety," Peter said.

Isabel shot him a glare. Her whole world was being turned upside down. Now there were four people against her: her parents, the bishop, and the detective. *Well, not exactly against me*, she told herself, trying to come to terms with the situation, but she felt as if she had lost her independence. She no longer had a job, and now the very details of her life were being decided for her.

Peter pulled a cell phone from his pocket, and moved closer to Isabel. Her heart fluttered wildly and her breath came in short gasps. "I'll show you how it works," he said. "My number is already in there. All you have to do is sweep your finger across it at the bottom to open it, like this,"—he demonstrated—"and now it's open."

Their fingers touched for a brief moment, and Isabel was not prepared for the powerful jolt that ran through her. She kept her eyes averted, not wanting the detective to see the effect he had on her.

The detective was still talking. "Now, you can see how it works?

Isabel nodded, looking aghast at the sight of the cell phone. She had not gone on *rumspringa* and had never used a cell phone before.

"And my number is the only number in there. I've put it in *Favorites* to make it easier and faster for you to call me, in case of, err, well, should you need to call me in a hurry."

The full weight of the situation

settled on Isabel like a cold dark heavy blanket. *Should she need to call in a hurry*. Did the detective really think the *mann* would come for her as she was the witness? She shuddered involuntarily.

Peter made Isabel call him several times, to make sure she knew how to use it.

Finally, Isabel asked the question she had been dreading asking, for she did not really want to hear the answer spoken out aloud. "Detective, am I in danger?"

She saw a flash of concern pass

across the detective's face but he hid it just as quickly. "I don't know, Isabel. If it is Raines, the man you are convinced you saw, he is a dangerous man, but as he has a water-tight alibi, he may not risk, um, coming after the only witness."

"But as I'm the only witness, won't he want to..." Isabel's voice trailed off, and she was embarrassed to hear her own voice sounding so shaken.

To her relief, the detective shook his head. "No, *if* it is Raines, it will look suspicious if he does try anything, and he can rest on his alibi."

"What if it isn't the same *mann*?" her *vadder* asked, his voice full of concern.

Peter Stutzman shifted in his seat. "Your daughter is convinced it is the same man," he said. "What's more, the Identi-Kit image was the same as the Raines' image."

"Would you like to stay for dinner?

Everyone turned to look at Mrs. Slabaugh. The question had come out of the blue.

"Thank you, Mrs. Slabaugh, but I

had better be getting home. Thank you so much for your time." Peter stood up, and looked down at Isabel. "Are you sure you know how to use the cell phone now?"

Isabel nodded.

"Please remember to keep it on you at all times, no matter what."

Isabel nodded again and watched her *vadder* show the detective to the door. Part of her was pleased he was leaving, but part of her was sorely disappointed that he had not accepted her *mudder's* invitation to stay for dinner.

CHAPTER 8

TWO DAYS LATER, Isabel was sitting
with her parents after dinner
playing the card game, *Dutch Blitz*.
The wind blew outside, turning the
blades on the ancient windmill
which sat near the equally ancient
barn. Both of them were once
painted red, but now most of the
paint was coming off in long strips,
or had already done so. The blades
whined and whistled as they
turned, but Isabel and her *mudder*
and *vadder* were so used to it that

they barely registered it.

"*Ach*, did you hear that?" Isabel's *mudder* jumped suddenly. She was a short and portly woman, contrasting with her tall and thin husband.

Isabel looked at her mother. "What? Do you mean Blessing whinnying loudly? I've never heard him do that before."

Her *mudder* shook her head. "*Nee*, I thought I heard something else. I don't mean Blessing; I just thought he was stirred up by the wind. I mean I thought I heard a car."

Isabel's father stood, and moved to the large window in the family room. He bent at the waist, and peered out into the darkness.

"I don't see anything," he said in his deep voice. He reached up with his thin but hardened fingers and tugged at his gray *baard*.

"Well, it's dark," his wife said from her chair. "You aren't likely to see anything, not from in here at any rate."

Before her *vadder* could answer, Isabel heard Blessing whinnying again, and then another sound. It sounded like a step on the front porch creaking. Everyone held their breath, and then another sound came. It sounded like someone trying to open the locked front door.

Isabel was glad, after all, that there were now locks on the doors. They had never had locks on their doors before, being in a peaceful Amish community, surrounded by their fields of corn and wheat and vegetables. Their closest *Englisch* neighbor was the kindly John Burns, a man in his eighties whose wife had died five years earlier.

Beyond that, it was six or so miles before they would run into anyone else.

After Isabel had seen the murderer flee, she had not felt safe, but at the same time, had not truly accepted the fact that she might be in danger. But now, hearing the step creak and the door handle move, her blood ran cold.

Isabel's heart pounded in her chest so hard that it blocked out sound. It beat in her ears so firmly and resoundingly that she missed what her *vadder* and *mudder* were saying until she noticed their lips were moving. Then she forced herself to calm down. She drew a deep breath, shut her eyes, and focused on what they were saying.

"I'm going to see who's there," her *vadder* was saying.

"*Nee, nee*, you're not." Her *mudder* clutched at his arm.

Isabel's father shook his head and made his way into the living room. Her mother rose from beside her and rushed after him. Isabel was rooted to the spot in fear. Then Isabel heard the lock snap open and her *mudder* speaking loudly.

"*Nee, nee*, Jonas. You can't go out there!"

"I must; I need to see who is sneaking around my *haus* at night."

"And do what?" Her *mudder's* voice was tense.

"Speak with him. Ask him to leave."

"*Nee*. Get Isabel to call the detective." Her mother's voice was trembling.

Isabel stood suddenly and picked up the cell phone from the table.

Her father nodded. "Go ahead," he said. "Give him a call."

Less than thirty minutes later, headlights shone through the living room window. In that thirty minutes they had not heard any more noises, and Blessing had stopped whinnying, but everyone was tense and on edge. Isabel's *vadder* was first to rise when the lights splashed across the wall, but the two women followed him to the front door.

He peeked out of the window and then unlocked and opened the door. Detective Stutzman soon burst through the door. He was dressed for work in a gray suit, with the jacket blowing behind him a bit as he walked briskly. His hand was on his hip, resting on the butt of his gun. He hurried into the *haus*, his face filled with concern.

"Thank you for coming, Peter," Mr. Slabaugh said, "but you're going to need to leave your gun in the car. As you know, we don't allow weapons in our *haus*."

"Oh yes, please forgive me," he said.

When Peter returned to the porch,

he was welcomed inside. He stood just inside the door and smiled softly to Isabel.

"Are you all right?" he asked her. His voice was full of tenderness and concern. When Isabel nodded, he continued. "You heard noises, and someone was trying to get in?" the detective asked the family at large.

"*Jah*," Isabel's father said. "Mary thought she heard a car, and then we heard someone walk up the porch steps, and then he tried the door handle."

"He was probably trying to scare you," Peter said. "If he had really wanted to get inside, he would have waited until your gas lamps were off, and waited until the middle of the night. Jonas, come with me and we'll have a look around, and you ladies stay inside. Lock the door behind us."

The men went outside to search the grounds together. The women stayed inside, with the front door locked, but Isabel's mother peeked out through the window, holding a curtain aside.

When the men finally returned,

everyone went into the living room, to the warmth of the fire.

"Someone was here," Peter said, holding his hands in front of the fire and rubbing them together. "We found tire tracks just off the drive some ways up, and footprints here and there. They should keep until morning, when I can get a team out here to run some plaster molds. I can run them, see if we can get anything useful from them."

Isabel did not know what to say; the idea of someone walking around her *haus* and trying to get in was all too much for her. She held a hand to her chest as Peter continued to speak.

"I'm going to stay on your couch tonight. I won't bring my gun in, but you need someone here just in case."

"*Nee*," Isabel said, without thinking. She was not sure why she was so opposed to the idea, and in truth it intrigued her a bit. Yet to have this *mann*, who at the same time both infuriated her and attracted her, on the couch, brought up too many conflicting feelings within her.

"I need to keep you safe," he said in an insistent tone that brooked no argument. "If this is about what you saw, if someone wants to keep you quiet, they aren't going to stop."

Isabel's *mudder* clutched at her throat. "Is that what you think this is? Is someone going to come for her?"

"It seems as if someone has already come," Isabel's *vadder* said. "If Detective Stutzman thinks he should stay, then he's going to stay."

And just like that it was settled. Her father sent Isabel upstairs to fetch some blankets and pillows from a closet for Peter. She carried them in her arms down the stairs. She could overhear her parents talking in the kitchen, and when she returned to the living room, only Stutzman was there.

Isabel's cheeks burned red. She was embarrassed that he would see she was so flustered. She moved to the couch and dumped the blankets and pillows upon it. She turned to leave without a word, but Peter stepped forward and took her softly by the arm, pulling her back around to face him.

"What are you doing?" Isabel asked, her eyes wide.

"I just wanted to let you know that I'm not going to let anything happen to you. Whoever is doing this, Raines, or anyone else, I won't let them get to you."

Isabel took a breath. "Why don't you think it was Raines?"

"I don't think Raines is the guy you saw, because we have him on video at the same time the murder happened. His lawyer has his waiting room on tape. Raines went in well before the murder, and came out a while after the murder. He was in there for the whole time. That doesn't mean I don't think he's involved, of course; he could've hired someone."

"It is him, I tell you," Isabel said. "The picture!"

Peter sighed and shook his head. He let go of Isabel's arm. "We don't have to have this conversation again; we had it a couple of days ago. We can't go after him, not with an alibi like that, not with him on tape. We just can't. If it is him, somehow, or if he's involved, we have to play it smart. If he's coming here, or sending someone, we can get him. We'll run those tracks tomorrow, and we'll pull it against any cars we know him to own, or his friends. There are footprints, so we'll have the type of shoe worn. This will give us a lot of openings to figure out what exactly is going on. All right?"

Isabel nodded. She felt as if she wanted to say something else, but instead she shook her head softly and went up to bed.

In her bed she lay under the covers and stared at the ceiling. The waxing moon was fat and almost full outside, a big silver orb hanging in the sky. It threw moonlight into Isabel's room, sending light across her floor, up and over the bed. Isabel looked to the moonlight, and watched it inch slowly along her covers as the moon floated lazily in the sky. She thought of the fact that someone had come to her *haus*, someone who she was convinced was out to hurt her. She thought of *Gott* and

His protection, and she also thought of Peter, and how much safer she felt knowing he was downstairs.

She closed her eyes and tried to quiet the thoughts that were running through her head, keeping her awake. Eventually she did, and she drifted off to sleep.

* * *

Detective Peter Stutzman made himself as comfortable as he could on the faded, blue couch, his knees bent so that he could fit without his feet hanging over the edge. Why was he so attracted to the girl? He knew that the Amish believed that God had chosen one man for every woman, and if he were Amish right now, he would believe without any doubt whatsoever that Isabel was the girl for him. But right now, he wasn't Amish; he was *Englisch*.

This was odd; he barely knew her. Yet she produced in him an overwhelming urge to protect her, to take her in his arms and make her safe.

To make matters worse, he wanted nothing more than to kiss her, to feel the touch of her soft lips upon his. *You're crazy, Peter*, he said to himself as he closed his eyes and tried vainly to get to sleep.

CHAPTER 9

IT WAS THE SECOND SUNDAY that the church gathering was held and this Sunday it was at Rebecca and Albert Stutzman's *haus*. Isabel was pleased to be going to the gathering. She always felt safe amongst a large gathering of the community; it was as if *Gott* was right there amongst them and nothing could hurt her.

Isobel saw Melissa standing by herself and hurried toward her.

Melissa and Isobel always sat with each other at the gatherings.

"*Hiya*, Isobel." Melissa leaned over to peer into Isobel's face. "My, you look dreadful. Didn't you sleep last night?"

Isobel shook her head. "*Nee*, I've had trouble sleeping ever since… Well, you know."

Melissa's face was filled with concern. "I know. Have the police found the person who did it yet?"

"*Nee*, I don't think so. They would've told us if they had."

Normally at the Stutzmans' place,

in warmer weather the gatherings were held out in the barn, but on this occasion, they had all their furniture moved out of the *haus* and all the wooden church benches fitted in close rows down the center of the *haus*.

Melissa and Isobel sat in the back row on the women's side. As always, it was the *menner* on the one side and the women on the other. During the half hour of singing, Isobel started to feel her old self again.

In fact, the *Loblied*, "Hymn of Praise," which was always the second song sung at every Amish church meeting - no matter which community one was in, this was always the second song - lifted her spirits as it always did.

O Lord Father, we bless thy name,

Thy love and thy goodness praise;

That thou, O Lord, so graciously

Have been to us always.

Thou hast brought us together, O Lord,

To be admonished through thy word.

Bestow on us thy grace.

O may thy servant be endowed

With wisdom from on high,

To preach thy word with truth and
power,

Thy name to glorify.

Which needful is to thy own praise,

Give hunger for thy word always,

This should be our desire.

Put wisdom in our hearts while

here

On earth thy will be known,

They word through grace to
understand

What thou would have us to do.

To live in righteousness, O Lord,

Submissive to thy word,

That all our vows prove true.

Thine only be the glory, O Lord,

Likeness all might and power.

That we praise thee in our

assembly

And feel grateful every hour.

With all our hearts we pray,

Wilt thou be with us every day

Through Christ our Lord. Amen.

The words seemed to lift the heaviness off her heart until it was clear and light. Isobel turned and smiled at Melissa just as the first minister was about to speak. With that smile she told Melissa she was feeling better. She knew that Melissa would be able to read her smile, since the two of them were as close as *schweschders*. Melissa gave her a big smile right back.

A minister stood up in front of them and began his preaching. He was a large man with thick, dark hair and a large, bushy, dark *baard.* His voice boomed right through the Stutzmans' *haus.* He spoke on forgiveness and how everyone should forgive one another as *Gott* has forgiven them.

Isobel noticed that Melissa was distracted by something. She followed the direction of Melissa's gaze and noted that Melissa was looking over at the other side of the room, at her new husband, Victor. Isobel wondered whether she would be so in love when she married. She hoped she would be, but she had never known what love was. She loved her *familye* and her animals, but she knew the love of a *mann* would be a far different thing and she ached to know what that was like. Seeing the look in Melissa's eyes whenever she talked about Victor gave Isobel an inkling of what it would feel like to be in love. *It must feel dreamy, comforting, and happy all at the same time*, she thought. *Just like I feel about the detective.*

With that thought, Isabel jumped in her seat, so strongly that Melissa turned to her and raised her eyebrows.

Isabel was aghast, and forced herself to take her mind off love and to turn her attention to what the minister was saying about forgiveness.

She realized it would be easy to forgive someone for a small transgression or some type of injustice, but how was Mrs. Harrison to forgive the person who murdered her husband? Just as that question popped into her head, the minister unknowingly answered it with his next words. "We use *Gott's* strength and not our own." Isobel wondered how one would go about using *Gott's* strength. It sounded *gut* in theory, but it seemed as though it would be much, much harder to do in real life.

When the minister finished, another minister spoke and then the bishop delivered the long sermon. Finally, a long prayer was said by Thomas Wyler.

After the church meeting had come to an end, the people moved to the side to enable the men to erect the long trestle tables for the after meal.

"That was *gut* today, wasn't it?" Melissa asked.

Isobel agreed, but wondered if Melissa had actually been listening or whether she was too busy looking at her new, handsome husband.

Jakob hurried over. "Isabel, I'll drive you to the Singing tonight."

Isabel bristled. Why didn't Jakob

ever ask her instead of telling her? "*Nee*, Jakob. *Denki*, but I don't want to go to the Singing tonight."

Jakob's cheeks puffed and his face reddened. "Isabel, can I have a word with you in private?"

Before she could answer, he took her elbow and moved her away from Melissa.

Isabel looked back at Melissa, who had raised her eyebrows and was trying not to laugh. "How dare you insult me!" he hissed.

Isabel was taken aback. "Insult you? Whatever do you mean?"

"You dared to turn me down in front of your friend."

Isabel was furious. "Leave me alone, Jakob." She hurried back to Melissa.

"Don't worry, he's gone outside," Melissa said before Isabel could turn around. "What was that all about?"

"Well, he seems to think he owns me and can tell me what to do."

Melissa scrunched up her face. "That's strange! You've only been on two buggy rides with him, although I suppose he's always hanging around you at Singings and the like."

As the two women stood to the side of the room, talking, the elderly Alice Byler came toward them and clung onto Isobel's hands. "Isobel, I heard your *Englisch* employer was murdered, is that right?"

Throughout the church meeting, Isobel had tried to put it out of her mind. She was finally starting to feel her old self, and the last thing that she wanted was to be reminded of the terrible thing that happened. Couldn't she just have a little break away from it all? Isobel forced a smile. "*Jah*, it was a terrible thing and I'm trying to put it out of my mind."

"*Nee*, you can't put it out of your mind," Alice said.

"Why can't she?" Melissa moved a little closer by Isobel's side.

Alice looked around about her and leaned forward to the two girls. "I heard that it's the Stutzmans' son who's investigating the case." Her tone was conspiratorial.

Isobel gasped as she put the pieces together: Rebecca and

Albert Stutzman were Peter's parents! She shot Melissa a startled look, and Melissa returned her a look just as startled. She had not told Melissa the name of the young detective.

"He's their son?" Isobel asked.

"*Jah,* he is their son," Alice Byler whispered, looking around her once again.

It was then that the memory of what had happened to the Stutzmans' other son came flooding back. Why hadn't she remembered this before? Bill

Stutzman had been accidentally killed some years earlier by a teenager who was robbing a store. Bill had been in the wrong place at the wrong time.

Isobel had heard that the Stutzmans' 'other son' had left the Amish because his parents had not wanted to do anything to avenge their son's death, instead saying it was '*Gott's* will.'

A vision of Peter Stutzman came into her mind. Was that why he left the Amish and joined the police force? He must have been of the opposite opinion to his parents and thought that they should have done something about their son.

He must be filled with pain, Isobel thought. *Pain of losing his bruder and being helpless to stop it. In an effort to feel in some kind of control of life, he joined the police force.*

"Did you know Peter Stutzman, Alice?"

Isobel was not surprised when Alice nodded.

"*Jah*, I knew him," Alice said. "You wouldn't remember him as he was about five or six years older than you. He was a delightful boy, but he changed when his *bruder* died. He screamed at his parents and challenged them to do something, but they would not."

"Is he the detective on the case, Isobel?" Melissa asked.

Isobel nodded and knew that later, she would have to explain to Melissa why she hadn't mentioned him. Then she decided now was as *gut* a time as any. "I didn't know he was Rebecca and Albert's son. I didn't even know that he had been brought up Amish." *It's quite a shock*, she thought.

Alice looked around about her yet again, still clutching onto Isabel's hands. "Best not to mention their son to them. I dare say they're upset about him leaving the community."

"*Denki*, Alice." Isobel watched Alice walk away. This time, Alice had given her useful information rather than the empty gossip she usually gave out.

"So, what's he like, this Peter Stutzman? And why were you keeping him a secret?"

Isobel laughed. "Oh, Melissa, I

wasn't keeping him a secret. Like I just said, I didn't even make the connection until just now when Alice told me who he was."

"I bet he's handsome, isn't he?" Melissa chuckled.

Isobel shrugged her shoulders and hesitated to answer.

Melissa patted her shoulder. "I'm sorry, I was only being silly. I know you've had a big shock."

Isobel wasn't listening to Melissa; she was too busy looking at Mr. Stutzman, who was helping the other *menner* arrange the tables.

Peter did look a lot like his *vadder*.

Isobel wondered what Peter's

bruder had been like.

CHAPTER 10

ONLY DAYS LATER, word came that old Eli Stutzman had passed away, and Isabel's first thought was sadness for his grandson, Peter.

When Isabel and Jakob pulled up to the Stutzmans' *haus* for the viewing, people were already making their way steadily inside. The people, all dressed in black, filed into the *haus*, holding their heads down. No one engaged in conversation at any great length, keeping only to the appropriate, "*Hullo.*"

The Stutzman home was a large and immaculate *haus*. In the spring and summer time, it glistened among the other houses in the community with its lush green lawn, white picket fence, and yellow sunflowers that lined the path to the doorway. Now, deep into the Lancaster winter, the *haus* seemed to have adopted a dark, gloomy feel. It had been only days since Isabel had stepped through the doors of the Stutzmans' *haus*, and suddenly an uneasy feeling swept over her.

As Isabel climbed down out of the heated buggy, the frigid air struck her, taking her completely by surprise. She stepped heavily and almost sank into the thick ice as she made her way clumsily towards the *haus*.

"You're shivering. I told you to bring your thick coat," Jakob said loudly as he caught up with her after tying up his horse. "Don't you remember that I instructed you to get your coat when I called for you, but you said it wasn't necessary?"

Instructed me? Isabel bit her tongue. Jakob was becoming increasingly infuriating, but now was most certainly neither the time nor the place to have an awkward conversation with him. Why on earth she had ever agreed to go with him to the viewing was simply beyond her.

She had at first thought Jakob to be kind and genuine, and for a long time had even entertained the thought that this was the *mann* she was going to marry. However, all that changed after she spent time in his company. He was arrogant, demanding, and at times, even rude. Being with him for any length of time always left her drained and frustrated.

She had begun to see a different side of Jakob. He told her he did not approve of her having a job working for *Englischers*, and that he did not approve of her close friendship with Melissa, as his *mudder* had told him that Melissa's *familye* members were too free with their ways. To make matters worse, Jakob had become increasingly possessive, controlling, and argumentative.

Now, Isabel longed for the solitude of working alone in the Old Candle Store. She missed the freedom of meeting up with Melissa at their favorite café at her leisure, and she missed not having to answer to anyone apart from her parents. Everything had changed since that fateful day when she had witnessed the *mann* running from the scene - and the day that she had met Detective Peter Stutzman.

Now, as they headed towards the Stutzmans' *haus*, Isabel fervently wished once more that she had not agreed to accompany Jakob there in his buggy. She'd had a headache when he had shown up at her *haus* and all but insisted he drive her there, and at the time, it had seemed the path of least resistance.

Despite the icy road, Isabel walked briskly and tried her best to make her way into the *haus* ahead of Jakob. She decided that she would ignore him for as long as she possibly could. Jakob's nagging voice was ringing inside her head and she longed for a peppermint tea.

As she reached the porch, once

again she heard Jakob's vexatious tone. "You know, you never listen to me when I tell you something. I told you to bring a coat, I knew it would be freezing. But as usual you never listen. You're so stubborn, Isabel."

"Jakob, this isn't a good time to start an argument. Can we discuss this after? What difference does it make anyway? We're already here and I did *not* bring the coat." She turned away from him, trying hard to keep both her voice and temper down.

Isabel walked into the *haus* ahead

of Jakob. The living room had been cleared of all furniture, and church benches had been brought in. People were sitting on them, speaking in hushed voices.

Others who were waiting to view the deceased were already in line, filing past the handmade, plain, pine coffin in the viewing room. The coffin was placed on a sturdy board between two high-backed, wooden chairs. Isabel took her place in line. Jakob leaned over her, too close for her comfort. *I'm going to have to make it very clear to him that I won't date him any more*, Isabel thought, *and at the very first opportunity*. The very thought brought release and she felt as if a huge burden had been lifted from her.

The coffin had six sides, with two sections on hinges that folded down to reveal the body from the chest up. The body was dressed in white pants, a vest, and a shirt.

Isabel turned and headed for her *mudder*, her steps quickening in an attempt to put distance between herself and Jakob. Her plan was thwarted by Alice Byler. The elderly woman gripped Isabel's arm, her long, bony fingers closing painfully. "Come and sit with me in the corner." Isabel followed meekly, grateful to have escaped Jakob, at least for the moment.

"The Stutzmans' son was just here, you just missed him," she hissed.

"Peter?"

Alice nodded. "*Jah*."

Isabel was puzzled. She had not thought through that problem: Peter, now an *Englischer*, attending the Amish viewing of his Amish *grossdawdi*. "Did his parents mind him being here?"

"*Phsaw*, of course not," Alice exclaimed, albeit quietly.

Isabel frowned. "But I thought you said that he didn't get along with his parents."

Alice shook her head. "*Nee*, he was angry with them when his *bruder* died, and left the Amish. He was close to his *grossdawdi*, and he often came here to see him, and visit with his parents too."

"He did, err, he does?" This was news to Isabel.

"*Jah*, they are hoping he will return to the Amish."

"That's not likely to happen."
Isabel wished she hadn't spoken
before thinking, as she would not
like her words repeated.

Alice readily agreed. "He has too
much root of bitterness and
unforgiveness in his heart. His poor
mudder, Rebecca, is always
praying for him to return to us, but
I can't see it happening." She
looked around the room furtively
as she spoke. "Rebecca gets her
hopes up as Peter often speaks to
the bishop."

One surprise after another, Isabel
thought. Aloud she said, "Why

would he speak to the bishop?"

Alice shrugged, and her eyes glinted. "Perhaps he is talking through the issues of forgiveness." She shrugged. "Only *Gott* and Peter and the bishop would know for sure. Yet mark my words, if he hasn't returned to the Amish yet, he never will." Alice cackled and made her way across the room, leaving Isabel alone.

Isabel's stomach churned and she felt as if her heart were wrenched within her. *If only Peter would return to the Amish*, she thought, as a wave of warmth engulfed her.

Melissa's husband, Victor, had returned to the Amish after some years, so it was a possibility, if even a remote one. Yet Peter seemed quite firmly *Englisch*, and filled with unforgiveness. She would have to continue to fight her feelings for him.

CHAPTER 11

THE FOLLOWING DAY was the funeral service and burial, and Isobel still had found no opportunity to tell Jakob that she no longer wished to date him. Thankfully, she had driven home with her parents in the *familye* buggy after the viewing of the day before, and had not seen Jakob since.

The funeral service was to be held at the Stutzman home, as the *haus* was large enough to accommodate a good number of people.

The service started with a minister reading - for there was no singing at Amish funerals - Hymn 144 from the *Ausbund*:

Listen all Christians, who have been born again,

The Son of God's from the Kingdom of Heaven died on the cross and suffered death and shame.

Let us follow Him! Let us take up our cross!

The blood of Jesus washes away the sins of those who leave,

All to follow Him,

And who believe on God alone,

Even though they have sinned much.

The minister then spoke for half an hour and reminded everyone present that their thoughts should not be on this world, but rather, on the world yet to come. He was followed by another minister, who spoke on Genesis, and how man came from dust and shall return to dust. He concluded by reciting *First Corinthians* chapter fifteen, verses twelve to nineteen:

"Now if Christ is proclaimed as raised from the dead, how can some of you say that there is no resurrection of the dead? But if there is no resurrection of the dead, then not even Christ has been raised. And if Christ has not been raised, then our preaching is in vain and your faith is in vain. We are even found to be misrepresenting God, because we testified about God that he raised Christ, whom he did not raise if it is true that the dead are not raised. For if the dead are not raised, not even Christ has been raised. And if Christ has not been *raised, your faith is futile and you are still in your sins. Then those also who have fallen asleep in Christ have perished. If in Christ we have hope in this life only, we are of all people most to be pitied."*

Then the minister spoke on forgiveness. He explained that forgiveness is not instant; rather, it is a journey which requires help from *Gott*. One must make a conscious decision not to hold onto unforgiveness.

Isabel thought of Peter Stutzman. He held unforgiveness in his heart, unforgiveness for his *bruder's* killer, and unforgiveness that his parents had forgiven the *mann* who had accidentally killed his *bruder*. If only Peter were here to hear this sermon. Or was he? Isobel had not seen him when she had taken her seat, but that did not mean that he was not already seated with the *menner*, or at the back of a room somewhere, listening. She sent up a silent prayer to *Gott* that the minister's message would somehow be brought home to Peter. It was the very message that he needed to hear.

An hour and a half to two hours later, the minister mentioned Eli Stutzman's name, date of birth, and date of death. That was the only time that the deceased had been mentioned throughout the entire service, as was Amish custom.

After the service, the people made their way out of the *haus* to head to the Amish cemetery. Snow was beginning to fall, and Isobel brushed some flakes from her eyelashes. Isabel spotted her parents, and hurried over to them when she saw that Jakob was coming up behind her. Isabel was going to the cemetery with her parents in their *familye* buggy, but she wanted to tell Jakob that she no longer intended to date him first. Isabel sighed at the thought. "*Mamm*, can you wait there for a moment, please? I just want a quick word with Jakob."

Her *mudder* raised her eyebrows, but did not speak.

Jakob caught up with her, and had overheard her words to her *mudder*. "Come on, Isabel. You can speak to me in the buggy on the way to the cemetery."

Isabel winced at Jakob's demanding tone, but walked away from the buggies so no one could overhear her. "Jakob, I'm just going to come out and say this. I don't want to date you any more. Sorry, but that's the way it is." Isabel was relieved that she finally said the words.

"You're kidding, right?" Jakob's voice was loud.

"*Nee*, I am not." Isabel made her voice as firm as she could. She saw that Jakob's face had turned a particularly unpleasant shade of red. She almost expected steam to come out of his ears. "And now, if you will excuse me," she continued, "I will travel to the cemetery with my *familye*."

Isabel walked towards her parents' buggy, hoping that Jakob would not follow her. As she turned her back to Jakob, a strong, chill wind blew the leaves off the tall oak trees outside the *haus*. Isabel turned her head away in the direction of the field to avoid the frigid breeze. As soon as she turned her head, her heart stopped. There, leaning against a bare, winter tree was a tall

Englischer in a black suit, white shirt, and black tie. It was Detective Peter Stutzman.

From across the road, he stared directly into Isabel's eyes. His gaze was so intense that it made Isabel uncomfortable, but she could not look away, try as she might. Her heart raced frantically. *Has he been watching me this whole time?* she asked herself. His penetrating gaze never wavered for a second. She shivered, but it was not from the chill winter breeze—she was reeling from the effects of Peter Stutzman's powerful gaze.

CHAPTER 12

THE COFFIN WAS PLACED in the hearse, which looked similar to a normal buggy, only it was bigger, box-like, and rectangular. It led a long line of buggies out to the Amish cemetery, one of around twenty in the county.

When Isabel joined her parents in the *familye* buggy, her mind was still across the field with Peter. She engaged in conversation, yet with a sense of detachment. Her life had been calm and quiet, but now it was as if she were caught in a fast river and she was hard put just to keep afloat.

As her parents drove to the little cemetery, Isabel spoke up. "I've broken up with Jakob."

"*Gut, gut,*" her *mudder* said quietly.

Isabel looked up, surprised. Her *mudder* hadn't wanted her to date Jakob? They had never spoken about it. Isabel was relieved.

As soon as Isabel hopped down from the warmth of the buggy, she was startled by a voice behind her. "Are you ready?"

Isabel whipped her head around to see Jakob standing behind her, his hands behind his back, and a serious look on his face.

"You're here," she said, turning to face him, surprised.

"*Jah*, why wouldn't I be?" He raised his eyebrows.

Isabel groaned inwardly. Was Jakob going to pretend that they were still dating, as if she hadn't meant what she had said? Isabel turned back to her *mudder*, and took her arm. Her *mudder* caught on at once, and promptly led Isabel away from Jakob.

The grave had already been dug by hand by *menner* of the community. The pale, stone tombstones were small and all of equal size. As this was an older cemetery, some of the stones had German writing on them, but most were in English. Each stone stated the deceased's name, as well as their birth date, date of death, and their age in years, months and days. There were no flowers in Amish cemeteries.

Everyone bowed their heads for the silent prayer, The Lord's Prayer, but before Isabel closed her eyes, she looked around for Peter. All she could see were bare trees that flanked the cemetery, their branches white with snow, and the tall grain silos in the distance.

The coffin was placed in the 'rough box,' an outer wood structure. The pallbearers, four widowed *menner*, lowered the coffin into the grave by ropes, and then the pallbearers and the *familye* filled the grave with dirt as the bishop read a hymn. Again, as was the custom, there was no singing. The bishop read part of Hymn 21 from the *Ausbund*:

The people were surprised. They said, "What is this? They go to death willingly, even though they could be free." Gotthard answered, "We do not die. Death just leads us to heaven where we shall be with all of God's children. We have this as our sure hope. Therefore we enter the gates of death with joy."

The service at the graveside was as short as the funeral service had been long, and before long, Isabel was traveling back to the Stutzmans' *haus* for the funeral meal.

Isabel and her *mudder* had spent the previous afternoon baking, and had delivered the food that morning, before the funeral service in the Stutzman *haus*. By the time they reached the *haus*, the food was already laid out: cold beef, chicken pieces, mashed potatoes, gravy, coleslaw, pepper cabbage, freshly baked bread, applesauce, cheese, and the raisin-laden *funeral pie*, as well as the hard *funeral biscuits*, cookies made from caraway seeds, sugar, butter, flour, and pearl ash.

Once inside, Isabel took off her coat and followed her *mudder* into the living room, where several members of the community had already gathered and were sipping hot meadow tea.

"I have to go to the bathroom," Isabel said to her *mudder,* once they were settled inside. As she made her way upstairs to the bathroom, she looked around for Jakob, but to her relief, he was nowhere in sight. Perhaps he had really gotten her message when she had spoken to him sternly after the service, or perhaps he was so angry that he didn't want to cause a scene in front of everyone. Regardless of what was going in his head, she was grateful that it was finally over between them.

After Isabel left the bathroom, she headed back down the stairs to rejoin her *mudder*. As she was at the end of the corridor and just about to turn the corner, a hand seized her arm and pulled her into a dark room. She was about to scream when a voice whispered, "It's okay, it's me, Peter," in her ear. Her knees went weak with relief. For a moment, she had thought it was the *mann* she had seen fleeing from the Old Candle Store.

"Come with me," he said, before he opened the door, peeped around the corner, and pulled her back into the corridor behind him.

Peter led her back down the corridor, and down another set of stairs that led to the laundry room. "Sorry about that, but we need to talk in private," he said.

"You scared me!" Isabel had not

meant her tone to come out as such an accusation, but she truly had been sacred.

Peter looked contrite. "I'm sorry," he said, "but it was unavoidable. I just needed to take you away from there, because I have some further information, and I can't be seen talking to you."

Isabel was breathing heavily and shaking. The laundry room was freezing. She cast a glance around it. It was clearly used for canning as well as laundry. An old hand-cranked wringer-washer stood in one corner, next to a more modern wringer-washer that was run by a little diesel motor. The exhaust pipe ran out the open window.

Peter must have followed her gaze, for he at once moved to the window, removed the exhaust pipe, and shut the window. Peter took off his jacket and wrapped it around Isabel. She shook even harder from his nearness, but snuggled into the comforting warmth of his jacket. It smelled like him, all woodsy cedar and sandalwood soap.

Isabel had never wished that Peter were Amish more fervently than she did at this moment. She longed for him to pull her into his arms, and she wondered once again what the sweet taste of his lips on hers would be like. Isabel shook her head as if to clear such thoughts.

Could Peter ever return to the Amish? That was their only hope of any future together, assuming he wanted one too, of course. Isobel suppressed a giggle. She was getting way ahead of herself here. Isabel thought this over for a moment, and then remembered why they were there. "What did you have to tell me?" she asked.

Peter looked a little embarrassed. "I'm not supposed to tell you this, but you were right after all. You did see Raines. Our investigation has turned up some information about his lawyer. Turns out that his lawyer isn't the fine, upstanding citizen that everyone thought."

"I told you I saw Raines," Isabel said triumphantly, but then added, "What does this mean, for me?"

"I don't know at this stage." Peter's eyes crinkled up at the corners with concern. "It should be okay, if the lawyer doesn't find out that we're onto him. You should be safe from Raines so long as he thinks we're buying his alibi."

"And if he doesn't?"

An unmistakable look of concern passed over Peter's face. "Well, you just let me worry about that."

CHAPTER 13

Isabel thought that over. She was enjoying her talk with Peter, despite the circumstances. He made her heart tremble, and caused a thousand butterflies to churn around in her stomach.

Isabel pulled Peter's coat more tightly around her. It comforted her, although she did not know if she should be wearing *Englisch* clothes, so cast her gaze around the room in her nervousness. She noticed clothes strewn about the tiny room and clothes in the sink. There were *Englischer* clothes hanging from pegs to dry.

"Are you staying here, with your parents?"

"*Jah*," Peter said, and then stopped speaking when Isabel gasped at his use of Pennsylvania Dutch. He shrugged and then continued. "Only until this matter is all sorted out. I'm closer to your house should anything happen."

"I didn't know, until I heard today, that you still spoke to your parents." Peter looked uncomfortable, so Isabel at once apologized. "Please forgive me, I shouldn't have said anything. It's none of my business."

Peter shook his head. "It's all right. After Adrian's death, I didn't speak to my parents for some years. I feel so bad about it now, it was as if they lost both their *kinner*. It used to be hard for me to be around my parents. I couldn't get over the fact that not only had they forgiven Adrian's killer, but they pleaded for him to be placed in juvenile detention instead of going to jail. They said that he needed rehabilitation. My *bruder* was dead because of that young *mann* and my parents begged for leniency. Of course, I was told at the time that he had not meant to kill my *bruder*, but had struck at him while trying to escape, but I was too full of bitterness. My *bruder* was gone, and that's all that counted."

Isabel heard not only the hurt, but also the anger in Peter's voice. Now she was witnessing first hand just how much his *bruder's* death had affected him. She wanted to hold him, hug him, comfort him, and show him how much she cared, but of course it was not her place. Instead she asked, "Is that why you became a detective?"

Peter nodded. "Yes, it was. I believed that criminals needed to pay for what they had done. That young *mann* ripped my *familye* apart. I joined the police with the intention of bringing everyone I could to justice. I was a very angry *mann* back then."

For a brief moment they were both were quiet. "And now?" Isobel asked. "Can you find it in your heart to forgive him?"

Peter opened his mouth to reply, but the words never came, for at that moment, they were interrupted by an angry voice.

"Isabel! Are you in there?" Isabel jumped at the sound of Jakob's demanding and hostile tone, and then Jakob burst through the door. "I've been searching for you for a long time."

"We have nothing to speak about." Isabel's voice was firm.

Jakob looked taken aback, and looked Peter up and down before turning to Isobel. "You should not be in a room alone with a *mann*."

Peter calmly pulled out his badge and held it up to Jakob. "Police business," he said dryly.

Isobel was upset, upset with Jakob for humiliating her, and upset that he had interrupted the important conversation she was having with Peter.

Isabel handed Peter's coat back to him, and hurried through the door, with Jakob trailing along behind her. "I was starting to get worried," Jakob said, his voice harsh.

Isabel turned around and faced him squarely. "How dare you, Jakob! How dare you spy on me, and how dare you speak to me like you did! I told you, it's over between us! Don't you dare ever follow me again, do you hear me?" With that, she stomped her foot, and hurried back down the corridor.

CHAPTER 14

ISABEL DROVE BLESSING to Melissa's *haus*. She had not seen much of her friend of late, apart from the recent funeral and the Sunday church meeting. When Isabel had worked at the Old Candle Store, she and Melissa had met at least once a week for lunch, although it was often more frequently. How her world had been turned upside down in such a short space of time! She remembered the Scripture in the book of James that said, "You do not know what tomorrow will bring." *How right that is*, she said to herself.

As Isabel approached a little lane running off the main road, she debated whether to turn off or take the road directly ahead. The black clouds were rolling in thick and fast, signaling that a storm was brewing. The wind was picking up, and Isabel thought perhaps she should stay on the main road for once. Both roads were of equal length, but the little lane was far more picturesque. It was a narrow lane that the *Englischers* did not take, much less know about, but today, there would be no point in taking the scenic route. Isabel just wanted to get to Melissa's, and fast before the storm came. Little pieces of sleet were already biting into her face.

Isabel made to go past the lane when, much to her shock, Blessing suddenly reared. Before Isabel could think what to do, he spun on his haunches, turned sharply, and bolted away from the road and down the little lane. Isabel fought for control, and managed to stop him soon enough, under the spreading but bare branches of a massive white oak tree on the top of a little hill.

"Whoa, whoa, Blessing. Whatever has gotten into you? You've never done that before." Isabel was trembling.

Blessing snorted and stamped his foot. Isabel held him still for a moment under the shelter of the tree, to calm him, but at that moment, saw a car traveling slowly on the road below. Isabel peered through the stinging sleet. The car was going slowly, much more slowly than a car would normally go. The weather wasn't pleasant, but it wasn't bad enough to cause a driver to go anywhere near that slowly. It was a black car, with tinted windows, so she was unable to see anyone inside.

Had the car been following her? Did the driver think she was still just ahead? If Blessing hadn't bolted, she would in fact have been on that very road, just ahead of the car.

Isabel shuddered violently. She shook the reins and pushed Blessing on as fast as she dare go, and headed straight for Melissa's *haus.*

Isabel drove straight through the wide doors of the large barn and unharnessed Blessing, who appeared to have calmed down and was back to his usual self. Isabel put him in a stall next to Melissa and Victor's buggy horse, Herman. The two whinnied happily at each other.

Isabel took Blessing's dark green, heavy stable blanket out of the buggy, and then hesitated for a moment before deciding that the blanket was sufficient. Had Blessing been outside, he would have needed his thick, turnout, winter waterproof blanket, but the barn was snug and warm. Isabel was trembling so much from the encounter with the car, that she had trouble doing up the dees on the blanket.

Isabel had sewn a pocket into her dress to hold the cell phone. As a rule, Amish did not have pockets, but she had to keep the cell phone on her at all times. It was well out of sight, under her over-apron.

Isabel now took the phone out of her pocket and looked at it. Should she call Peter? She wanted to, even if just to hear his voice, but then silently scolded herself. The cell phone was strictly for police business, to be used only if she was threatened or felt under threat. Still, Peter had insisted that she call him, even if something only slightly suspicious had happened.

Isabel had never used a cell phone before. As she slid her thumb across the bottom of the screen just as Peter had showed her, and then pressed his name in *Favorites*, she sent up a silent prayer to *Gott* to apologize for the thrill that using the phone had given her.

Peter answered at once. "Are you in danger?" he barked.

"*Nee, nee.*" Isabel hurried to reassure him. "I didn't know whether to call you or not, but I've just arrived at my friend Melissa's *haus* and I think I was followed."

"You were followed there?" Peter's tone was urgent.

"*Nee, nee,*" Isabel said again. "I turned off into a lane and the car went straight ahead."

Peter let out a long sigh of clear

relief. "Are you sure they didn't see you?'

"*Jah*, as sure I can be. I actually didn't intend to drive down the lane, and I was going straight ahead, but my horse took fright and suddenly turned down the lane and galloped for a bit until I could stop him. I held him still under a tree to calm him, and that's when I saw the car on the lower road. It was going very slowly, as slowly as someone who thought they were following a buggy would go."

"Description?"

Isabel scratched her head. "It was a big, black car, with dark windows."

"Tinted windows?"

"*Jah*, very dark, I couldn't see anyone inside."

"And I suppose you were too far away to make out the plates?"

"*Jah*." Isabel at once felt a little silly for calling Peter. "Peter, I'm sorry I called you."

"Not at all." Peter's voice was firm. "I would've been very upset if you hadn't called me. Do me a favor, would you?"

"What?"

Peter chuckled. "You're supposed to say 'yes,' not 'what.'"

Isabel smiled, her stomach doing flips at Peter's laugh. "*Nee*, I don't know what the favor is yet."

Peter's voice reverted to seriousness. "Call me one hour before you leave Melissa's, and I want you to drive one of their horses home. Leave Blessing there."

Isabel was puzzled. "Sure, I'll call you, but why ever not drive Blessing home?"

"His color stands out too much. He's a palomino, and I don't know of any other palomino buggy horses in these parts. Driving him makes you instantly recognizable, so if you were driving a bay or even a chestnut, you would just blend in with all the other Amish."

Isabel had to agree. "That makes sense. But what if Melissa drives Blessing? Won't they think that she's me?"

"Make sure you tell her that she must not drive him. I'll collect Blessing for you and drive him to your house in an open buggy in broad daylight tomorrow, if the weather clears, but for now, leave him where he is, and make sure no one drives him."

"I will."

"Oh, and Isabel?"

"Yes?"

"Please be careful. I'd be…" Peter hesitated before continuing in a soft voice, "very upset if anything were to happen to you."

After the conversation, Isabel leaned back against a pole in the barn, her heart racing so hard that she felt it would burst through her ears. A warm, tingly feeling ran from the top of her head right down to her toes. *He really cares for me*, she thought. Her happiness was not even dampened by the dangerous situation in which she found herself.

CHAPTER 15

As soon as Isabel reached the door, Melissa opened it with a squeal of delight. "Isabel! Quick, come inside to the fire! It's freezing out there," she said.

Isabel followed her friend into the living room, where a roaring fire was blazing. As the two sat, warming themselves by the welcoming fire, sipping hot meadow tea and nibbling peanut brittle, Isabel told Melissa of the morning's events. As she progressed, Melissa looked more and more shocked.

"*Ach*, Isabel, that's so *schecklich*!"

"I suppose it is scary, Melissa, but I don't feel scared, to tell you the truth."

Melissa shot her a knowing look. "It's because of that handsome detective, isn't it?"

Isabel's face grew hot and she ducked her head.

Melissa chuckled. "I knew it!"

"Oh, Melissa, I really do like him,

but what can come of it? He's an *Englischer*. What I am to do?"

Melissa frowned. "Well, Victor came back to the Amish."

Isabel shook her head. "But you said that Victor had been thinking about it for a long time. And it's not often that a *mann* does return to the Amish after he's been away for so long. Plus, Peter has all those feelings of unforgiveness over his *bruder's* death."

"Trust in *Gott*," Melissa said. "Gott verlosst die Seine nicht." *God does not abandon His own.*

"I think it's more that Peter has abandoned *Gott*," Isabel said.

Melissa shook her finger at her. "*Nee, nee*, you don't know that, Isabel. From what I've heard, Peter is already back in touch with the bishop, and he's reconciled with his parents. He has one foot in the Amish door already."

Isabel sighed. "He needs two feet in the Amish door, as you put it, if anything is ever to happen between us."

Melissa just shrugged. "It doesn't seem as bad to me as it seems to you, I'm sure. Anyway, I have some corn draining. Come and help me make corncakes. We can have them with maple syrup."

"And marshmallows?"

Melissa laughed. "Of course, I always have marshmallows on hand for you, Isabel."

The two friends walked into the kitchen, where Melissa took a pot of boiling water from the wood cookstove, while Isabel poured some cornmeal, honey, and salt into a large bowl. Melissa walked over and added the drained corn kernels and the boiling water, and then Isabel stirred.

Melissa beat the whites of two eggs, and then folded them though the mixture. Soon the two were spooning the mixture into a griddle.

Less than ten minutes later, the girls were back by the fire, eating corncakes laced with maple syrup and topped with marshmallows. Isabel felt safe by the comforting fire. How lovely it would be to be married to Peter, sitting by the fire in their own *haus*, and raising *bopplis*. Her face flushed and her ears burned at the thought.

Yet something was standing in their way: unforgiveness. The ministers often quoted First Peter, chapter four, and verse eight: "Love covers a multitude of sins." Could love help Peter to forgive?

CHAPTER 16

ISABEL WAS NERVOUS. When Peter had driven Blessing back in Victor's open topped buggy, her *mudder* had invited him to stay for dinner. He had agreed, and Peter was right now speaking to her parents in the living room, while she was checking on the Six Layer Dinner.

Isabel paced up and down the kitchen. Peter and her parents were getting on well together. They were all speaking in

Pennsylvania Dutch rather than in *Englisch*. It was as if Peter was already back with the Amish. But he was not, and that was the issue.

Isabel could not allow herself to let her feelings run away with her. She was heading for heartbreak, of that she was certain. Sure, Victor had returned to the Amish, but what were the chances that Peter would?

Isabel wrung her hands together, and sent up a silent prayer. "*Gott*, please help Peter overcome the unforgiveness and bitterness in his heart."

"Isabel, why are you taking so long?" Her *mudder's* voice startled her.

"Sorry, *Mamm*, just checking on the Six Layer Dinner."

Her mother frowned at her. "Is it ready?"

Isabel nodded. "*Jah*."

Soon the four of them were seated at the kitchen table, and, after the silent prayer, were all tucking into the layers of beef, potatoes, tomatoes, green pepper, onion, and celery of the delicious Six Layer Dinner.

"I saw Jakob at Samuel Beiler's Coach Shop today," her *vadder* said out of the blue. "He was getting new fiberglass wheels fitted to his buggy."

Why on earth would her *vadder* mention Jakob now, and especially with Peter present? Isabel was mortified. She sank down lower in her chair.

"How is Samuel?" Mrs. Slabaugh asked her husband. "He looked quite pale and ill at the last church meeting."

Mr. Slabaugh shrugged. "Now that

you mention it, he didn't look his usual self. Anyway, back to Jakob."

Isabel groaned inwardly. Whatever would her *vadder* say next? To make matters worse, Peter made no secret of the fact that he was keenly interested in the conversation. He had stopped eating and had put down his fork.

"Jakob was not very friendly to me," her *vadder* continued. "I expect he's still taking it hard that you two are no longer courting."

"You're not?" Peter blushed as everyone turned to look at him.

"*Nee*," Isabel said, looking down at her fork in her embarrassment. "I broke it off with him at the funeral meal."

Peter appeared to be trying to hide a smile, and was not doing so successfully at all.

"And just as well," Mrs. Slabaugh snapped. "I did not approve."

Isabel's forehead creased into a deep frown. "You didn't? But you didn't say anything, *Mamm*." Things were going from bad to worse. Her parents were discussing personal matters in front of Peter.

This was strange, but even stranger was the fact that they appeared to approve of Peter, who was still an *Englischer*. Isabel shook her head to try to clear the thoughts that were all tumbling into her head, one after the other.

At any rate, her parents must have thought they had said enough, for there was silence for the moment. Isabel hoped nothing further would be said to embarrass her, but only minutes later, her *vadder* turned to Peter.

"So, Peter, do you intend to stay as an *Englischer* for the rest of your earthly life?"

Isabel gasped, and so did her *mudder*. "Jonas!" her *mudder* exclaimed.

Peter winced, and shifted in his chair. "*Nee*, that's all right," he said to Mrs. Slabaugh. Turning to Mr. Slabaugh, he said, "I have been talking to the bishop for some months now."

No one spoke. It was clear to Isobel that Peter was avoiding the question, and she hoped that her *vadder* would not push him on it.

"*Gut, gut*," Mrs. Slabaugh said,

clearly as an attempt to cover up what she obviously considered to be her husband's rudeness.

"And what did the bishop say?" Mr. Slabaugh finally asked.

Isabel saw the glare that her *mudder* directed at her *vadder*, but her *vadder* seemed intent upon getting an answer.

Peter scratched his head and then let out a long sigh of resignation. "The bishop says I have to forgive. I have been working on forgiveness, but it isn't coming easily."

"Is that all that's standing in your way, then, son?" Mr. Slabaugh said.

Mrs. Slabaugh simply shook her head and went back to eating her food, while Peter squirmed in his seat.

"Matthew chapter six, verse fifteen," her *vadder* said. "'*But if you do not forgive others their trespasses, neither will your Father forgive your trespasses.*'"

"Scripture smart!" Mrs. Slabaugh hissed her disapproval.

Unperturbed, Mr. Slabaugh pressed

on. "And Mark chapter eleven and verse twenty five says, '*And whenever you stand praying, forgive, if you have anything against anyone, so that your Father also who is in heaven may forgive you your trespasses.*' But of course, you know all that."

Peter sighed long and loud. "*Jah*, I do know all that. I was brought up knowing that, as a follower of Jesus Christ, I would have to accept suffering as He accepted suffering. The bishop has lately helped me to understand that my own troubles are insignificant when

I picture Jesus on the cross."

Mr. Slabaugh nodded.

"And now I do believe that I have forgiven the young *mann* who killed my *bruder*," Peter continued, "but as for returning to the Amish, have I gone too far? I am a police officer; I carry a gun. That is against everything we believe in. I could give that up in an instant, but have I gone too far away from the community to be able to return?"

Mr. Slabaugh shook his head. "'*Nor height, nor depth, nor any other created thing, will be able to separate us from the love of God, which is in Christ Jesus our Lord,*" he quoted. "'*All we like sheep have gone astray; none is righteous, no, not one.*'" It was Mr. Slabaugh's turn to shift in his seat, as, judging by her stern face and the clearing of her throat, Mrs. Slabaugh was clearly not pleased that he was being *Scripture Smart* by quoting so many Scriptures. Doing so was considered prideful.

"No one has ever gone too far from *Gott*," Mr. Slabaugh continued, "as I am sure the bishop has told you."

Peter nodded. "I know all that in theory," he said, "but it's hard to take it all in."

"Just trust in *Gott*," her *vadder* said. "Do not make it too complicated."

Isabel was a little embarrassed, sitting there and listening to the meaningful conversation between Peter and her *vadder*. When everyone had finished their Six Layer Dinner, she cleared the plates, refusing her *mudder's* offer of help.

In the kitchen, Isabel took the

tapioca pudding from the gas refrigerator and added butter and marshmallows to the top, and then reached back into the refrigerator for the Molasses Oatmeal Pie in shortcut pie crust.

Isabel reached into her pocket for the cell phone, which she had gotten into the habit of doing, as it made her think of Peter. With a gasp she realized it wasn't there. When had she last had it? Isabel thought for a moment. She remembered having it in the barn. After Peter had brought Blessing back, she had put him in his stall and fed him. She remembered having it then. It must have dropped out of her pocket. *Nee,* she remembered leaving it out near Blessing's stall when she threw him some hay. What if it had fallen into his stall and he'd stomped on it and broken it?

Isabel looked out the kitchen window. She would not need a lamp, as the moon was full and bright, and there were no clouds in the sky. Without a second's thought for her own safety, Isabel rushed out the back door and headed for the barn.

CHAPTER 17

As Isabel walked nervously to the barn, the hair on the back of her neck stood up. Wave after wave of uneasy sensations washed over her. Her breath came in jagged gasps. Suddenly, she had the eerie sensation that she was being watched. Isabel clutched at her throat and wondered whether she should run back to the *haus*. *Nee*, surely she was only being silly. She was letting her imagination run away with her. It had been silly of her to leave the security of the *haus*, but she had made it this far, so might as well go on. Just a few more steps, and she would have the cell phone, which hopefully was still in one piece.

Isabel reached the barn and turned on the gas lamp just inside the door, and then everything happened in a blur.

She felt a bee buzz past her head and wondered why a bee would be out on such a cold night. At the same time, she heard a man scream.

Isabel gingerly edged forward. Blessing was out of his stall. That was no surprise, as Blessing was known to open gates, but what was a surprise, was that he was sitting on a *mann*.

Isabel's first thought was that Blessing was hurt. "Blessing!" she called as she ran to him, but then she tripped. Looking down, she saw that she had tripped over a gun, and the realization slowly dawned on her that the man had shot at her. It had been a bullet, not a bee. Still, there was no time to worry about that, as she was concerned for Blessing. She ventured closer to see if Blessing was all right, but he appeared to be not only unhurt, but pleased with himself, as he sat on the *mann* who looked remarkably like the photo of Clifton Raines.

"Isabel!" The voice was Peter's, and was full of blind panic.

"I'm okay, I'm in here," she called.

Peter and her *vadder* appeared at the door to the barn, followed soon after by her *mudder,* who was breathless.

"He shot at me," she said, "but

Blessing knocked him down and he's sitting on him."

Peter put one arm around her shoulder and pulled her so tightly to him that she could scarcely breathe, but then he released her and bent down to pick up the gun.

"Did you hear the gunshot?" she asked him.

He shook his head. "*Nee*, it has a silencer on it. We came because you called. I saw your caller I.D. and was worried when you didn't speak."

Isabel was puzzled. "Called?"

"*Jah*, you called Peter's cell phone," her *vadder* said.

"*Nee*, I didn't," Isabel said. "I remembered I'd left the cell phone near Blessing's stall earlier tonight so I came to fetch it."

"Isabel, you shouldn't have done something so irresponsible as coming out here," Peter said in a shaky voice. "Jonas, where is some rope?" Soon the two men had Blessing off Raines and were tying up the man. Peter also tied a strip of cloth across Raines' mouth, as he was saying some mighty unpleasant things.

Isabel checked Blessing, but he appeared to be fine. Peter called for backup, and then apologized to Isabel. "I'm sorry I snapped at you earlier. I just couldn't bear it if anything happened to you."

Isabel noticed that her mother smiled and looked away. "I didn't call you," she said as an afterthought. "That is strange."

Peter laughed. "There's your answer." He pointed to Blessing, who had the cell phone in his mouth. There was a loud crunch, and it broke in two. Isabel hurried into the stall to retrieve it.

"I'm so sorry, Peter," she said, as she handed him the remaining pieces of the phone. "Blessing does like to put things in his mouth."

Peter laughed. "Don't worry, we won't be needing that phone any more. I'd say Blessing must have picked it up before, and somehow accidentally called me. I was the only number in your phone."

"*Jah*, I suppose that must be it." Isabel could think of no other explanation.

"The three of you go to the *haus* now, and I'll wait here with Raines for the uniformed officers, and then I'll call at the *haus* before I leave."

The three of them did as they were told. Isabel was happy to be back in the warmth of the *haus*, but she and her parents were shaken. Why, she had been shot at, and she could have been killed. She was pleased that her parents did not scold her for going out to the barn. She could not believe she had been so thoughtless as to do such a thing - it was such a silly thing to do under the circumstances.

It seemed to take forever for Peter to return to the *haus*. Isabel was sitting by the fire, sipping on hot cocoa.

No sooner was Peter through the door, than Mrs. Slabaugh asked a question. "Now that you have the *mann* out there, does it mean that Isabel's safe now?"

"I have a bit of a plan," Peter said, not directly answering the question. "We will tell Raines' lawyer that some harm has come to Isabel, and say we can't find Raines. The lawyer and Raines have no doubt already cooked up another fake alibi for Raines. This way we'll have the lawyer, too. Once we have them both arrested, you will be perfectly safe, Isabel."

Isabel was relieved, but part of her wondered if she would ever see Peter again. Overwhelming sadness suddenly struck her.

Peter was still speaking. "I'll call back here tomorrow"—at that, Isabel's heart sang—"and update you on what's happened. Meanwhile, I don't want the three of you to speak to anyone, anyone at all. Don't even answer the door, no matter who it is. We have to keep this quiet for the moment. Don't worry, it should be all over soon, possibly by midday."

With that, Peter left, leaving Isabel staring after him. After tomorrow, would she ever see Peter again?

CHAPTER 18

Isabel awoke before the sun, or rather, before dawn, as there was no sun today; a howling wind was bringing with it driving snow. She had gone to bed with Peter on her mind, and had woken up with Peter on her mind. Was there any future for them? She dearly wanted there to be, but it all depended on Peter. She knew he cared for her, but was he in love with her? And even if he was, could he ever return to the Amish?

No doubt, Isabel would find out that very day. She felt sick at the thought. Isabel dressed and went down to breakfast, even though she had no appetite whatsoever. Her *mudder* was already awake, and was serving scrapple, along with eggs and fried potatoes. Preserved fruits and cereal were already on the kitchen table.

"Would you like me to cook some oatmeal, *Mamm*?"

Her *mudder* shooed her away. "*Nee*, sit! You've had quite enough of a shock. Here, drink this *kaffi*."

Isabel gratefully took the *kaffi* and sipped it, enjoying the warmth flowing though her. "You're up even earlier today, *Mamm*."

Her mother sat opposite her and rubbed her forehead. "Yes, I found it difficult to sleep. The whole *familye* has had quite a shock."

"I'm sorry, *Mamm*."

"It's not your fault, Isabel. You have nothing to be sorry for."

Isabel simply smiled. She enjoyed sitting there, safe and protected and warm. She could not imagine life outside the Amish. But what about Peter? He had lived as an *Englischer* for so long; were the ways of the world so firmly entrenched in him that he would not be able to put them behind him?

The morning seemed to drag on forever. Isabel mopped the floors and then set herself to baking. By midday, there was still no sign of Peter. Isabel's *vadder* came inside for lunch and the three ate a hearty meal together—or rather, Isabel's parents ate, while Isabel picked at her food. Where was Peter?

After Isabel's *vadder* went back outside, Isabel peered out the window every few moments. After what seemed an age, she finally heard the sound of a car. Isabel ran to the window. She saw Peter get out of his car and walk into the barn.

Isabel's *mudder* came over. "Is Peter here?"

"*Jah*, and he's gone to speak to *Datt*."

Her *mudder* simply shrugged and went back to her knitting. After a while, her *mudder* said, "Isabel, come and sit by the fire, you're making me nervous pacing up and down."

Isabel did as she was asked. "What can be taking him so long?"

A few moments later, her *vadder* and Peter came into the *haus*. "*Gut* news," her *vadder* said at once. He and Peter sat down next to each other on the old, blue couch.

"Raines and his lawyer have both been arrested," he said, "And what's more, they both confessed."

Isabel scrunched up her face as wave after wave of relief washed over her. "So your plan worked."

"It did indeed," Peter said with a twinkle in his eye. "When the lawyer found out that Raines was already in custody, he fell over himself to implicate Raines. He confessed to everything, but said that Raines had threatened him. Raines also confessed and said that it was all the lawyer's idea. They'll both be going to jail for a very long time."

"So I'm safe now?"

Peter nodded and his face lit up. "Yes, you're safe."

Mrs. Slabaugh beamed.

"*Wunderbaar*!" she said. "I'll make us all some hot meadow tea." Isabel rose to help, but her *mudder* waved her back to her chair.

As they sat and drank hot meadow tea and ate slices of shoo-fly pie, the two men discussed the legal proceedings. Mrs. Slabaugh seemed content with the fact that her *dochder* was now safe, and Isabel was wondering whether she would ever see Peter again. She caught herself biting at a fingernail, then wringing her hands, and then shifting in her seat. Peter did not seem to notice as he was engrossed in conversation with her *vadder*.

Finally, Peter stood up. Her parents thanked him again for his help, and then Mrs. Slabaugh went into the kitchen. Mr. Slabaugh said he had to get back to work, and so Peter and Isabel were left alone in the living room.

CHAPTER 19

ISABEL STOOD THERE, wondering if this was the final goodbye.

Peter walked over to her, and put his hands on her shoulders. His touch unleashed a flood of butterflies in her stomach. "Isabel, come with me now." With that, he headed for the door.

Isabel trailed after him, somewhat confused. "Oh, okay." She assumed she had to sign something, or give another statement. "I'll tell my parents where I'm going," she said as she caught up to him.

Peter shook his head. "I already told your *vadder*."

Isabel nodded. "All right, then." She took her heavy, black shawl from its peg, wrapped it around her, and then followed Peter to his car, happy at least that she would be with him a little longer.

Isabel looked over at Peter and saw he was gripping the wheel so hard that his knuckles were white. They drove off into the cold. Isabel fervently hoped that the snow would fall so hard that they would have to turn back, so she could be with Peter even longer. Yet the snow had stopped falling now, and Isabel looked out the window at the white landscape surrounding her. Black and white cows and snow covered barns dotted the beautiful rolling hills.

She was so engrossed with the loveliness of the winter scenery that at first she did not notice Peter turning down a little lane to the pond on the Stutzman farm.

"Aren't we going to the police

station?"

Peter chuckled. "*Nee*. Is that where you thought we were going?'

Isabel nodded, wondered where he was taking her.

"The pond was my favorite place to go as a child. I won't have this car much longer. I was only keeping it until your case was solved."

Isabel wondered why Peter was speaking about his car and why his voice was awash with nervousness.

"I don't have a buggy, not yet," Peter said, and Isabel's heart leaped at the word *yet*. Could this mean what she thought it meant?

"And so, please consider this a buggy ride," he continued, as he stopped the car.

A buggy ride? Isabel looked at Peter. Tingles filled her body as their eyes met, and the full import of his words sank in. *A buggy ride means a date.*

Peter reached for her hand. Isabel took it without hesitation, and their fingers entwined. Isabel's stomach clenched at the pleasurable feelings that his touch produced.

"Isabel, I've spoken to the bishop,

and I'm returning to the community. My *vadder* wants me to farm with him, and now that my *grossdawdi* has gone to be with *Gott*, I'm moving into my *grossdawdi's haus* on the *familye* farm."

A few shocks had come Isabel's way in recent times, but this one rivaled them all.

Peter's fingers tightened around Isabel's hand, causing her breath to come in short bursts. "I know we haven't known each long," Peter continued, his voice full of nervousness, "but I know you're the only woman for me. I've spoken to your *vadder*..."

"My *vadder*!" Isabel interrupted him, and her free hand flew to her throat.

Peter chuckled. "I asked him permission to ask you to marry me, and he gave it."

"Marry me?" Isabel exclaimed. She felt as if she were in a dream.

"Isabel, are you going to repeat everything I say for the rest of our lives?"

Peter leaned towards her, and his closeness set her pulses racing. He cupped her face in his strong hand, and Isabel caught her breath as she took in his masculine scent of sandalwood and lime.

Their lips met tenderly, but for Isabel, all too briefly. She shut her eyes as if to seal in the memory of his velvety lips on hers.

"I want to do this right," Peter said, stroking her cheek. "There will be a time for kisses later, a lifetime of kisses."

NEXT BOOK IN THIS SERIES

PATIENCE

THE AMISH BUGGY HORSE, BOOK 4

PATIENCE BEILER LEFT her community years ago due to a broken heart. Now, circumstances have forced her to return to the community. She finds herself unable to avoid Simon Warner, now a widower with two little girls, the man who caused her so much pain.

Can she break through the web of

lies and deceit that have conspired against her for years, and this time, find true love?

ABOUT RUTH HARTZLER

RUTH HARTZLER IS AN internationally best-selling and award-winning author of clean and sweet romance, including Amish Romance, Christian Western Romance, and Cozy Mysteries. Ruth is the recipient of several All-Star Awards (author and book).

www.ruthhartzler.com

35109358R10170

Made in the USA
Lexington, KY
01 April 2019